GRAVEN
IMAGES

GRAVEN IMAGES

3 Stories by

Paul Fleischman

ILLUSTRATIONS BY
ANDREW GLASS

SCHOLASTIC INC.
New York Toronto London Auckland Sydney

ISBN 0-590-43196-X

12 11 10 9 8 7 6 5 4 3 2 1   9/8 0 1 2 3 4/9

Printed in the U.S.A.   28

First Scholastic printing, September 1989

For Becky

Contents

The
Binnacle
Boy

1

WHEN THE BRIG *Orion*, three weeks out from Havana, appeared off her home port of New Bethany, Maine, Miss Evangeline Frye was just parting her bed curtains, formally banishing night.

While those who'd chanced to spy the sails wondered why the ship hadn't fired a salute, Miss Frye was combing her coarse, gray hair. While the *Orion* drifted unexpectedly about, at last presenting her stern to the harbor, Miss Frye was blowing the hearth fire into being. And while the harbor pilot's drowsy son rowed his father out to the ship, to return in a frenzy, eyes wide and hands trembling, Miss Frye was stationed at her parlor window, awaiting the sight of Sarah Peel.

She peered down the length of Bartholomew Street. Straight-spined as a mast and so tall that her gaze was aimed out through the top row of windowpanes, Miss Frye eyed the clock on the town hall next door. It was eight fifteen. The girl was late—and plenty of scrubbing and spinning to be done.

She pursed her lips, lowered her eyes, and looked out upon her flower garden. It was nearly Independence Day—tansy was thriving, pinks were in bloom, marigolds were budding on schedule. But the poppy seeds

she'd bought from a rogue of a peddler, and gullibly
planted with care, still hadn't sent up a single shoot.
And probably never would, she reflected. In memory,
she heard her mother's voice: "Girls take after their
mothers, Evangeline. Men take after the Devil." She
regarded the bare stretch of soil below, sneering at this
latest confirmation.

The door knocker sounded. Miss Frye opened up and
was surprised to find not Sarah Peel, but her ten-year-
old younger sister, Tekoa.

"I've come to do chores, ma'am."

Miss Frye cocked her head. "But where is Sarah?"

"In bed, ma'am. Taken ill." The girl spoke softly,
tucking a strand of straw-blond hair under her kerchief.

"Well then." Miss Frye motioned her in and closed
the door behind her. "I suppose you've had practice
scouring pewter."

Tekoa stood in the hallway, silent.

Miss Frye blinked her eyes. Was this some imperti-
nence? Then at once she recalled what Sarah had told
her—that the girl had been left deaf by a fever and
was able to listen only with her eyes, by reading the
words on others' lips.

Miss Frye passed Tekoa, then turned to face her.

"You can begin with the pewter."

"Yes, ma'am," said the girl.

Miss Frye led her down the hall to the kitchen. "And

what manner of illness has seized poor Sarah?"

"Her jaws," said Tekoa. "They won't come open."

Miss Frye appeared startled. "And when did this happen?"

"This morning, just after the news of the *Orion*."

Miss Frye's eyebrows jerked. "The *Orion*? What news?" Among the crew of New Bethany boys was Miss Frye's adopted son, Ethan.

"She appeared offshore this morning, ma'am," Tekoa calmly replied.

At once Miss Frye rushed to the window.

"All of the crew were found to be dead."

2

Bells were tolled. Trunks were opened and mourning clothes solemnly exhumed. The crew of the brig *Orion* was buried. And yet the matter remained unfinished.

No evidence of attack had been found. There was no sign of scurvy, no shortage of food. When the ship was boarded the crew was discovered to be lying about the decks as if hexed, with no witness to bear the tale to the living. None, that is, except the binnacle boy.

He alone remained standing, the life-sized carving of a sailor boy holding the iron binnacle, the housing for the ship's compass. Straight backed, sober lipped, in his jacket and cap, he stood resolutely before the helm, his lacquered eyes shining chicory blue. And after the ship's sails had been furled and her cargo of molasses unloaded, the binnacle boy was laid in a wagon and, like the seventeen sailors before him, slowly borne up the road to the top of the cliff upon which New Bethany stood. And there, before the town hall, the pinewood statue was mounted, still bearing the ship's compass, a memorial to the *Orion*'s crew.

Upon him the families of the dead gazed for hours, convinced he'd somehow reveal the nature of the catastrophe he'd witnessed. Mothers kept watch on his ruddy lips, expecting each moment to see them move. Fathers stared into his painted eyes, waiting to catch them in the act of blinking. Children cocked their ears to the wind as it moaned eerily over the boy, and believed they heard the sound of his voice.

Yet the binnacle boy clung to his secret. The mystery of the *Orion* remained, and gradually, as the summer progressed, those who stood and awaited the boy's words were replaced by those who'd come instead to leave him with secrets of their own, knowing his steadfast lips to be sealed.

At first it was children who took up the practice. After whispering into his chiseled ear, they ran off, or studied his stouthearted features as if expecting a nod of acknowledgment. Soon their elders took after them, and before long the binnacle boy became the repository for all that couldn't be safely spoken aloud in New Bethany.

Lovers opened their hearts to him. Hurrying figures sought him out in the night. Those who felt their lives running out entrusted him with their final confessions.

It was one of these last, a long-winded farmer, whom Miss Frye was observing from her parlor one morning when she noticed three women with parasols filing down the walk toward her door.

"Tekoa," she addressed her helper. "I believe we have company."

The brass door knocker sounded three times. Tekoa set down her feather duster, opened the door, and showed into the parlor Miss Bunch, Miss Mayhew, and Mrs. Stiggins.

"Good day to you, Miss Frye," chirped Miss Bunch. Without asking, she plopped herself down on a chair, a trespass that drew a stare from her hostess. Affirming her sovereign powers, Miss Frye regally motioned the others to be seated.

"It's some time since you've been seen about," said Miss Bunch. "So we decided to come on our own." She dabbed at the sweat on her brow with a handkerchief, adjusted her bonnet, and opened her fan. "To express our condolences, that is. About your son, Ethan."

"Indeed," said Miss Mayhew.

"You're very kind," replied Miss Frye. She noted that, like herself, Mrs. Stiggins was attired in a black mourning dress.

"I believe that your Ethan and my Jeroboam were *dear* companions," Mrs. Stiggins spoke up. "Aye, and full of mischief, as well."

"All boys be apprenticed to the Devil," said Miss Frye.

Tekoa entered with a pitcher of cider.

"And tell me, child," Miss Bunch addressed her. "How does your sister Sarah progress?"

"She's able to open her mouth, ma'am, and eat. But she's weak still, and refuses to speak to a soul."

"Truly now!" Miss Bunch lamented. "Come, child— sit down and visit with us."

Tekoa turned her eyes toward her mistress, who was glaring across at Miss Bunch in dismay.

"If you're fully caught up with your work," said Miss Frye, "you may take a chair, Tekoa, and join us."

The girl found herself a seat in the corner. And in the midst of the conversation Miss Bunch noticed Tekoa looking out the window.

She touched the girl's shoulder. "What do you see, child?"

"Excuse me, ma'am. Nothing of importance, ma'am."

"Nothing?" Miss Bunch lowered her voice. "You

were eyeing the binnacle boy, I warrant. Watching the ones that speak in his ear—same as *I'd* be doing myself if I knew the trick of reading lips." She glanced at Miss Mayhew and the two traded smiles.

"In truth, I was watching the swallows, ma'am."

"Swallows!" Miss Bunch commenced to chuckle. "*Any* fool can see swallows, child. But perhaps you'd put your eyes to use—and tell us what you next see spoken into the statue's ear."

Miss Mayhew's own dim eyes lit up.

"Really!" protested Miss Frye. "That's not proper!"

"Purely to help pass the time," said Miss Bunch. "To take our minds from our grief for a spell."

Tekoa stared at the women uneasily.

"And naturally," Miss Mayhew piped up, "with the curtains drawn, only she'll know who's speaking."

"And she'll *not* disclose the name," Miss Bunch added.

Miss Frye looked over at Mrs. Stiggins. Both knew that the matter wasn't right. And yet they too were curious as to what was said to the binnacle boy. After all, they themselves wouldn't actually be eavesdropping. And the name of the speaker would remain a mystery, never to be revealed.

"You may humor Miss Bunch's wishes, Tekoa," Miss Frye announced after deliberation.

"Yes, ma'am," said the girl.

The curtains were closed, dimming the light. Tekoa

reluctantly took up her post, while Miss Bunch and Miss Mayhew looked on in suspense.

The church bell declared it to be eleven. Then noon. Impatiently the women fanned themselves, squirming about like children in church. Then suddenly Tekoa drew back from the window.

"Did you spy someone?" Miss Bunch burst out. And suddenly it occurred to her that some sharp-eyed soul might reveal the fact that one of the various false teeth she wore had originally belonged to a dog.

"Yes, ma'am, I did."

Miss Mayhew grinned eagerly. "Well then—and what was spoken, child?"

The girl swallowed.

"Come now—speak up! Let us hear it word for word."

"Yes, ma'am."

Tekoa lowered her gaze. She studied her hands, and breathed in deeply.

" 'I know what killed the *Orion*'s crew.' "

3

After her three visitors had gone and Tekoa had finished her chores and left, Miss Frye climbed to the top of the stairs, and then, as she hadn't in weeks, turned right.

Tekoa's revelation still rang in her head as she walked down the hall, came to a halt—and opened the door to Ethan's room.

She stood there in the doorway a moment. The room was musty, the light dim. She passed his bed, opened the curtains, and gazed out his window at the indigo sea, musing on all he might have been.

Miss Frye turned around. Surveying the cobwebs, she recalled that both her natural sons had occupied the room as well. But they'd grown up wild, and long ago had left, following their father to sea, and like him gaining a fondness for the rum they freighted across the waters. When the schooner on which all three had shipped went down in a gale off the Georgia coast, Miss Frye had been neither surprised nor sorry, and had returned with relief to her maiden name. Her mother, herself abandoned by her husband, regarded the sinking as a fitting judgment. "Men," she'd summed up, "are a stench in God's nostrils."

Miss Frye paced slowly about the room. She found herself staring at Ethan's washstand, recalling the chill October day she'd gone mushroom picking, miles from home, and discovered an infant wrapped in a flour sack, left at a crossroads, dead. Or so she'd feared, till she'd gradually warmed him, holding the bundle next to her skin—and felt him slowly begin to squirm. Astonished, she hadn't known what to do, until suddenly something her mother had long ago told her leaped into memory: "If you save a creature's life, Evangeline, you're responsible for its every deed afterward." Unwilling to entrust his raising to another, she'd borne him home, burnt the flour sack, bathed him thoroughly, and named him Ethan.

Miss Frye walked up to his mahogany desk. The lamp by which he'd worked was dusty. His goose-quill pen and his ink bottle waited. She opened the primer he'd used, and recalled the pleasures of shaping his youthful mind.

A freethinker in religious matters, she'd refused to take the child to church and had taught him a catechism of her own devising. Shunning New Bethany's public school, Miss Frye had been his only tutor as well. She'd vowed that Ethan would turn out a gentleman, cultured and refined, an exception to his sex. No weed would be allowed to take root in the boy, no unwanted notion would enter his head. She would tend the child like a seedling tree, encouraging one branch and cutting another, keeping the image of its final shape fixed firmly in her mind. After all, she reasoned, God had meant him to die; by granting him life she'd assumed His role. The boy was thenceforward her private domain, whose growing body she marveled at as if it were her own work.

Tekoa's words came suddenly to mind and Miss Frye

emerged from her reverie. She closed the curtains, shut the door, and marched downstairs to the parlor again.

It was dusk. She stood watch on the binnacle boy, hoping to catch someone seeking his ear, desperate to know whom Tekoa had seen.

When the light at last failed she gave up her vigil and slowly sipped down a bowl of bean soup. She wondered if Tekoa might have made up the message she'd reported—then quickly put the thought out of her head. There wasn't a speck of deceit in the girl, and Miss Frye wondered what Tekoa must think of a mistress who ordered her to eavesdrop.

She broke through the crust of a cold plum tart and considered the girl's ways. She performed her duties competently enough, and yet there was something distant about her. The others had hopped to Miss Frye's commands and striven anxiously to please her. They'd always been afraid of her, as Tekoa's sister Sarah had been—little wonder, since of all the town, Miss Frye alone did not go to church. She rarely went out, and was rarely visited. Yet in her presence quiet Tekoa seemed to be calmly detached.

Hoping to break through the girl's silence, and frantic to know whom she'd seen at the statue, she called Tekoa from her work the next morning and set her to watching the binnacle boy. She felt a need to win the girl to her and hoped she was appreciative of this respite from her chores. Doggedly, she attempted to kindle a conversation with the girl, in vain. Thereafter Miss Frye sat in silence, studying Tekoa's pale features, hoping the speaker she'd seen might return.

For an hour Tekoa watched from the window. Then glancing over to her left she sighted Miss Bunch and her two companions, traveling under the portable shade of their parasols, bustling down the walk.

"Dear child—how good to see you," Miss Bunch addressed Tekoa at the door. "And good day to you as well, Miss Frye. As you're no doubt lonely without your dear son, we felt it to be our solemn duty to lend you our company once again."

"You're most kind," Miss Frye curtly replied.

"And while we're here," Miss Mayhew added, while Miss Frye led them into the parlor, "we thought Tekoa might be allowed to read out the secrets spoken to the statue."

"In quest of the truth concerning the *Orion*," Mrs. Stiggins sternly declared.

Miss Frye declined to mention the fact that she'd already had the girl doing just that. Ashamed to engage in the practice so openly, she decided to set Tekoa to spinning—when she glimpsed a woman crossing the street and heading toward the binnacle boy.

"Yes, of course!" she stammered. "Why—we owe it to the town!"

She hurried Tekoa back to her seat. A few moments later the girl turned around.

"Well?" asked Miss Frye. "Have you something to report?"

"Yes, ma'am," the girl gravely replied.

Mrs. Stiggins leaned forward. "Let us hear it, then, child!"

Tekoa lowered her eyes in embarrassment. " 'Miss Pike put no money in the collection plate at church, but only rattled the coins.' "

Miss Bunch and Miss Mayhew gaped at each other. A blush spread over Mrs. Stiggins.

"You may return to the window now, Tekoa," Miss Frye informed the girl.

In silence, the women fanned themselves. Mrs. Stiggins looked across at Miss Frye.

"My dear Jeroboam always spoke *most* highly of your Ethan."

Miss Frye gazed blankly, lost in thought. "He might have been a scholar. Or a poet, perhaps."

Slowly, Tekoa drew back from the window.

Miss Frye's eyes flashed.

"What is it? Something spoken?"

"Yes, ma'am."

"Well then—speak it out, Tekoa!"

The girl glanced down at the hardwood floor.

" 'Tonight we meet. Under the elm tree.' "

Miss Bunch gasped for breath. "*Which* elm tree, child?"

"Didn't say, ma'am," Tekoa replied.

Miss Bunch and Miss Mayhew sighed in unison. Again they waited while Tekoa watched.

"My Jeroboam had just turned fourteen," Mrs. Stiggins said. "And your Ethan?"

"Fourteen as well," Miss Frye replied.

Mrs. Stiggins released a sigh.

An hour passed. The church bell rang twelve. Miss Bunch yawned and reached for her parasol.

"Perhaps we should go."

"Indeed," said Miss Mayhew.

Suddenly, Tekoa turned. Her eyes appeared glazed, her features stiff.

"What is it?" Miss Frye demanded. "A message?"

"Yes, ma'am," the girl reluctantly replied.

"Gracious sakes, child—let us hear it then!"

Tekoa swallowed. She gazed absently before her.

" 'One of the tins of tea snuck among the Orion's provisions—was poisoned.' "

"*Poisoned?*" shrieked Mrs. Stiggins. "The tea?"

Miss Frye jumped up. "Is there more, Tekoa?"

"That's all of it, ma'am."

Mrs. Stiggins shot forward. "I insist you reveal the speaker," she cried, taking hold of Tekoa's shoulders.

"But ma'am, the agreement—"

"She's right," said Miss Bunch. "The name of the speaker must not be revealed."

"But my very own Jeroboam—poisoned! The murderer must be brought to justice!"

"Perhaps," said Miss Mayhew, "the speaker is lying."

Slowly, Miss Frye paced the room. "But why would someone lie to the statue?"

"No reason at all," Mrs. Stiggins snapped. She sat back down and wrung her hands. "They must have opened the tea that morning."

"And Lord knows," Miss Mayhew grimly continued, "with all the molasses they sweeten it with, they might have drunk hemlock itself and not known it."

A silence fell over Miss Frye's three visitors. They rose to their feet, bid farewell to Miss Frye, and slowly retraced their steps down the street, avoiding the binnacle boy's eyes in passing, as if this knower of secrets might discover their own with a glance.

4

Miss Frye did not sleep well that night. The next morning Tekoa's revelation still echoed in her ears. When the girl arrived at eight o'clock, Miss Frye set her to mixing up bread dough and stepped outside to the garden.

At a deliberate pace she strolled the paths, searching for comfort in the company of flowers. She smiled to see her larkspur thriving, and lad's-love blooming in its appointed season. She gazed upon her Queen Margrets and mint, and sampled the various scents of her roses.

Sitting on a bench, she inspected her tansy, eyeing the cornmeal-yellow petals and recalling how Ethan too had loved flowers. She grinned to remember the morning they'd merrily roamed the cliff, two summers before, collecting posies of hawkweed and chicory—and at once the smile left her lips. For that was the day the loquacious Mrs. Gump had stopped them to chat on their return. The woman's ill-mannered son had appeared, while she jabbered about her watery eye, and the pain in her lungs, and the history of her limp—till Miss Frye turned around to find the boys gone, dashing through Mrs. Gump's melon patch and trampling her corn, playing at pirates.

It was not till weeks later that Miss Frye discovered that Ethan was sneaking off in the evenings, to cavort with Mrs. Gump's son and others. When she'd confronted him he was unrepentant and had openly mocked her in Sarah's presence. Recalling her ship-bred, rum-sodden sons, she'd had no choice but to be stern with the boy, determined he'd bloom according to plan.

And now, she reflected, Ethan was gone, his promise lost forever.

Miss Frye marched indoors and entered the parlor, closed the curtains, and approached Tekoa. The girl was setting her dough to rise, and although Miss Frye knew there was mending to be done, she felt driven to find out if anything further about the *Orion* might come to light.

"Rest yourself awhile," said Miss Frye, "and aim your eyes on the binnacle boy."

The girl sat down and no sooner looked out than Miss Bunch, Miss Mayhew, and Mrs. Stiggins made their way to the door.

"Good day, Tekoa," bubbled Miss Bunch. "And good day to you, my dear Miss Frye. A day *especially* long for one so recently robbed of her child."

"Indeed," said Miss Mayhew. "The very reason we felt bound to help you pass the time."

Miss Frye's lips puckered. "How very thoughtful."

"Perhaps Tekoa could be of assistance," suggested Miss Bunch.

"If she's free," said Miss Mayhew.

Mrs. Stiggins tapped her parasol on the floor. "That justice might be done."

The women seated themselves in the parlor and Tekoa resumed her place at the window.

An hour passed in silent suspense, Miss Frye's three guests providing the barest minimum of their promised companionship.

"Tell me, Tekoa," Miss Bunch spoke up. "How does your precious sister fare?"

"The same, ma'am," the girl replied.

Miss Bunch shook her head and softened her voice. "I've heard it said that Sarah had a sweetheart among the *Orion*'s crew. Simeon Sprigg, they say it was." She glanced from one pair of eyes to the next. "They say the two were seen talking together, and that he's the cause of the girl's affliction."

Her listeners shook their heads in sympathy, then returned their attention once more to Tekoa.

Patiently, the girl looked out, though no one was near the binnacle boy. She trained her gaze on the swirling swallows and watched the swifts career through the sky. She studied a sparrow feeding its young—and suddenly noticed a figure appear, approach the statue, and seek out its ear.

"What is it, Tekoa?" Miss Frye demanded.

"Something spoken, ma'am. To the binnacle boy."

"Naturally, child! But what? Speak it out!"

Tekoa swallowed. She glanced about. Her lips quivered nervously.

" 'He wouldn't listen. He wished to roam free—and signed himself aboard the *Orion*.' "

Mrs. Stiggins bolted to her feet. "Quick, child—is this the same speaker as before?"

Gloomily, Tekoa nodded, and Mrs. Stiggins' eyes blazed.

"I *demand* to know who it is at once!"

Seeing the woman charging toward her, Tekoa clasped the curtains shut.

"Away, child!" Mrs. Stiggins ordered, as she grabbed a curtain—and flung it open.

"Sarah!" she gasped. "Sarah Peel!"

The others scrambled at once to the window.

"Protecting her older sister, she was!" Mrs. Stiggins shouted out. "But we'll get to the truth—believe me we will!"

Snatching her parasol, she steamed out the door, with Miss Bunch and Miss Mayhew right behind her.

"Tekoa—stay here and mind the bread!" Miss Frye settled a stern eye on the girl. Then quickly she followed her guests out the door, and found them standing in a circle around Sarah.

"So it's you!" thundered Mrs. Stiggins. "You—who can't get a word out of your lips."

"Except to the binnacle boy," said Miss Mayhew.

"And small wonder that your jaws seized shut." Mrs. Stiggins peered into her eyes. "With a secret like yours perched on your tongue."

Sarah lowered her gaze at once and fingered her long, brown hair.

"Namely," Mrs. Stiggins proclaimed, "that it was *you* who murdered the *Orion*'s crew!"

Sarah's eyes opened wide in terror.

"You couldn't bear your sweetheart Simeon Sprigg

forsaking you for the sea." Mrs. Stiggins poked the girl's shoe with the tip of her parasol. "So you poisoned him—and his mates as well!"

Speechlessly, Sarah shook her head, desperately denying the charge. Her jaws trembled, her lips twitched. She labored to open her mouth and speak, noticed Miss Frye's eyes upon her—and all of a sudden broke free.

"Seize her!" Mrs. Stiggins screamed.

Panic-stricken, Sarah dashed off, holding the hem of her skirt as she ran.

"She mustn't escape!" Miss Bunch cried out, and the four took after her in pursuit. Down the middle of the street they scurried, gathering the curious to their cause and shouting for those with fleeter feet to catch the girl at once. Panting, the women turned down an alley, and soon trailed the mob they'd called into being. Along the common, past the graveyard, through a field they hurried along, till they crossed a meadow and at last caught up with the rest of the crowd—at the cliff.

"And where's the girl?" Mrs. Stiggins demanded.

A man turned around. "Sarah Peel, ma'am?"

"Of course! And who *else*?" Mrs. Stiggins snapped.

"Fell from the cliff, ma'am. Drowned, she did."

Mrs. Stiggins gasped.

Miss Frye closed her eyes.

"Poor, dear Sarah," she whispered.

Side by side, without speaking a word, the women

slowly made their way homeward. Left alone for the final block of her journey, Miss Frye cast a glance at the binnacle boy, turned to her left, and approached his ear.

"Sarah spoke truly—he meant to go to sea. Not Simeon Sprigg, but my Ethan."

She paused for a moment. "Sarah must have seen." She licked her lips and drew closer to the statue. "That it was I who poisoned the *Orion*'s crew."

Miss Frye glanced across at her planting of tansy, with whose deadly leaves she'd destroyed her wayward son, and the corrupting crew as well. Dreamily, she stared at the flowers, yellow as the noonday sun—and so failed to notice Tekoa Peel remove her gaze from her mistress' lips, take a step back from the parlor window, and hurry toward the back door.

Saint Crispin's Follower

1

MR. SOLOMON QUINCE, master shoemaker, stood beside Nicholas, his fledgling apprentice, inhaled the spring air, looked up at the stars—and, ignorant of the constellations, found the sky strewn with the shapes of shoes.

"Well now, Nicholas, my lad," he said. "How does the ancient and honorable craft of shoemaking agree with you?" He sucked on his pipe and surveyed the heavens, picking out jackboots and brocade slippers.

"Very well," mumbled Nicholas. He cleared his throat. "Fine, sir."

His master smiled and savored the night. A moon lit up the great city of Charleston, capital of the colony of South Carolina, and threw Mr. Quince's portly profile onto the walk in front of his shop.

"A noble calling it is, Nicholas." Scanning the sky, Mr. Quince spied the shapes of gluepots and pliers and mallets and lasts. "Aye, and I wager you'll serve it well."

The shoemaker studied his lanky apprentice. The boy was thin as a wrought-iron picket, with a shirt that hung like a sail in a calm. His brown eyes were fixed on the distant stars.

"That is," continued Mr. Quince, "if you learn to leave off *daydreaming*—and buckle your brains to your work."

Nicholas started, and instantly disengaged his eyes from the heavens.

"You've got promise, lad—that's plain as a peacock. But you'll have to give up your moonin' about." Mr. Quince put a fatherly hand on his shoulder. "Look alive at your work! Keep your eyelids hoisted! Stay alert as a hare, lad—a hare chased by hounds!"

Nicholas swallowed uneasily and quickly straightened his posture.

"It's a worthy trade you've chosen, Nicholas. A glorious—an *exalted* trade." Mr. Quince lowered his voice to a whisper. "Do you imagine King George could do without shoes? Or the Turkish Sultan? Or the Empress of China?"

Mr. Quince disclosed a knowing smile.

"Nay, lad—they come to us. Crawling on their hands and knees!" Triumphantly, he puffed on his pipe. "And see that you're ready for 'em, Nicholas! Keep your fingers busy and your blinkers wide open. Give yourself to your work, lad, body and breeches—just like old Saint Crispin himself."

He gestured toward the weathervane on his roof, a hollow copper likeness of Saint Crispin, patron saint of shoemakers. Nearly as large as Nicholas and sporting a head of chiseled curls, the saint was shown sitting at his bench, his hammer upraised above a shoe.

"Always busy. Blinkers cocked on his work. Mark his ways, my lad—and follow."

Nicholas studied his patron saint. While the other vanes in sight pointed west, Saint Crispin was facing east at the moment, the result of a blow from a mulberry branch that had struck it during a hurricane. Believing, however, that the figure's main function was to advertise his shop, Mr. Quince had never bothered to repair it, untroubled that it looked east for days, then found itself stuck to the north, then the south.

"You've a friend there, lad. A friend and protector."

In wonder Nicholas gazed at the saint, who no longer tracked the source of the wind but noted instead, the apprentice fancied, other events, mysterious and sublime.

"Always watching over you, he is." Mr. Quince turned toward Nicholas. "So you needn't bother to busy your brains over anything but your work!"

Across the Ashley River came a breeze, bearing, as if to market, a cargo of jasmine and magnolia scents. Mr. Quince breathed in the fragrant air and raised his eyes to the stars.

"Let your thoughts never stray from shoes, Nicholas." Viewing the sky, he suddenly pulled the pipe from his mouth and gaped at the stars. "And your dreams as well, lad—always upon leather!"

Mesmerized, Mr. Quince peered at the heavens as though he were under a spell. Then abruptly he glanced at his apprentice, as if the boy might have found him out. For his eyes had discovered in the western sky not shoes, but the face of the woman he worshipped, the venomous Miss Catchfly.

"Aye, lad," he stammered, clearing his throat. "Shoe leather! Shoe leather and thread!"

"Shoe leather and thread," Nicholas murmured, forgetting the words at once. For he too was staring at the western sky, at the very stars Mr. Quince held dear, whose arrangement suggested no scrap of cowhide but rather the girl who worked at Miss Catchfly's grocery, for whom he pined in private—the comely Juliana.

2

The next morning Nicholas ambled downstairs, yawned mightily, swept the shop—and was at once dispatched by Mr. Quince into the sunlight on a round of errands.

Carrying a basket, he strolled down the walk, admiring the fine spring day. He passed Mr. Flinders' bookshop next door, where he often browsed when he had a free moment, and spotted the owner washing his windows in preparation for King George's birthday. Which, the apprentice suddenly recalled, would be celebrated the following day. Bells would be chimed, balls would be held. The ships in the harbor would fly their colors. The Charleston militia would march on parade and at night the town would glow like a bed of coals with the light of candles and lamps hung from balconies and set before windows.

Cheered by the thought of a holiday from work, Nicholas sauntered down the street. And following visits to the cutler, the baker, and Mr. McPhee, the beekeeper, he found himself standing before the door of the last of his stops, Miss Catchfly's grocery.

He looked through the window, and spied Juliana. His heart burst into a frenzy of labor. Collecting his courage, he flung the door open—and rammed it into the ladder from which Miss Catchfly, with broom, was doing battle with cobwebs.

"Thickwit!" she shrieked. "Jinglebrains!" She regained her balance and glared down at Nicholas. "Were you mothered by a *mole*, you blind-eyed oaf?"

Nicholas swallowed. "No, ma'am," he mumbled. In apology, he raised his gaze to her rose thorn nose and daggerlike chin. Then he noticed her shoes and spun quickly around, praying she wouldn't recall who he was. For the shoes had been made in Mr. Quince's shop— Nicholas remembered them at once. He himself had nailed on the heels—with tacks, he now feared, that *might* have been a sliver of an inch too long. Tacks whose tips might *possibly* sprout up through the soles with wear.

"Next time," spat out Miss Catchfly, "open your shutters and use your eyes!"

With relief, Nicholas returned his thoughts to the lesser of his crimes. "Yes, ma'am. I'll remember that, ma'am."

Miss Catchfly snorted and sneered. "I doubt it." Armed with her broom she slashed at the ceiling, vengefully laying waste to the cobwebs and causing a fleeing spider to drop onto Nicholas' back as he approached the counter.

"Three pounds of coffee beans, please," he stammered.

Juliana turned, in the act of pinning a sprig of honeysuckle to her bodice. Her skin was fair, her eyes deep green. Two amber curls danced on her forehead.

"Plus a loaf of sugar," Nicholas faltered. "And a half-dozen nutmegs—please."

Juliana turned and stifled a yawn, having lain awake most of the night inventing instruments of torture for the benefit of Winthrop Whistlewood, her faithless, and now former, suitor. Yawning again, she opened a jar, drowsily reached her hand inside and removed, by mistake, one nutmeg too many. While Nicholas nervously shifted his feet, Juliana emptied the nutmegs into his basket—and all of a sudden froze stiff at the sight of a spider climbing over his shoulder.

"Juliana!" Miss Catchfly stared at the girl. "Be your wits out to pasture? Look lively now, and finish filling the young man's order!"

Juliana gaped wide-eyed at Nicholas, then whirled around and fetched coffee and sugar. Unaware of the spider descending his shirt and breeches and scrambling across the floor, Nicholas paid for his purchases, turned, and set off out the door.

Dreamily, he walked down the street, meandering past the empty slave market, cocking his ear to a mockingbird's song. He stopped to gaze at a cypress tree and recalled the color of Juliana's eyes. Eyes, he mused, as green as keyholes through which one spied a field of clover. Then at once he remembered Mr. Quince's lecture—and awoke from his reverie. From now on he meant to keep his eyes skinned and his wits as sharp as the point on an awl.

He studied the passersby he met, scrutinizing their manners of dress and deducing their destinations. He noted the wind and appraised the clouds. He marked each carriage that clattered past. He looked down at his basket, inspected the sugar, counted the nutmegs— and found there were seven.

Nicholas stopped dead in his tracks. He counted again—and again found seven.

His eyebrows shot up. His thoughts whirled. He wondered if Juliana had merely miscounted—then he recalled the way she'd stared at him so strangely.

His heart fluttered. His mind spun like a top. Struck blind to clouds and carriages, he slowly digested the astounding truth: while Miss Catchfly was busy, and at great personal risk, Juliana had secretly given him an extra nutmeg—as a sign of her love.

In awe he examined the seventh nutmeg. He closed his eyes and sniffed it deeply. Entrusting it at last to his pocket, Nicholas drifted down the street while the amazing fact, flowerlike, gradually unfolded itself.

Juliana, he now realized, had only *appeared* to ignore him entirely every time he came into the shop. In truth, the girl was simply shy. Words did not come easily to her, so she spoke instead in the language at hand—the language of nutmegs and cornmeal and cloves.

Nicholas walked along in a daze, marveling at Juliana's courage—courage called forth on his behalf. Had Miss Catchfly caught her she'd have snatched her bareheaded. Why, that woman would just as soon bite herself as part with a shilling, or a speck of her flour. No doubt Juliana had planned the deed for days—or weeks, or even months!

Nicholas crossed a street, stopped, and plucked the nutmeg from his pocket. Hypnotized, he stared at it blankly, seeing in it, as if in a crystal ball, Juliana's image. Then all of a sudden his jaw dropped open.

She'd worn flowers—he recalled it clearly. Honeysuckle, he believed it was. And at once he thought back to a volume he'd opened in Mr. Flinders' bookshop one day—a volume devoted to the lore of flowers, including the meanings attached to them.

Instantly Nicholas took to his heels. Each flower, he recalled, bore its own sentiment. And undoubtedly Juliana hadn't worn just *any* bundle of petals, but had carefully chosen honeysuckle, out of all the plant kingdom, for the message it carried.

He reached the bookshop and charged through the door.

"Nicholas, my scholar—good morning to you!"

Mr. Flinders, bald-headed and bespectacled, lowered the book he was perusing point-blank. "Thirsting for knowledge as always, I see."

"Yes, sir," Nicholas answered quickly, aware that Mr. Quince was awaiting him. He glanced about, struggling to remember where he'd seen the book on flowers. Then he made a dash for a shelf in the corner.

"It's a fine thing to see a youth like yourself so ravenous for books and learning." Mr. Flinders gazed upon Nicholas as if beholding the hope of the future.

"Thank you, sir," mumbled the apprentice, desperately hunting the book.

"No doubt," asserted Mr. Flinders, "you spotted my notice in the *Gazette* and have come to inspect my latest shipment."

Combing the shelf, Nicholas gradually stooped out of Mr. Flinders' sight.

"You'll be glad to know that Pipkin's *Path to the Temple*

of Wisdom has come in at last."

Just then the apprentice ceased his search—and pulled from the shelf the book he sought.

"Plus a fine edition of Plutarch's *Lives*. And the works of Homer as well."

Nicholas hurriedly turned to the index. "Very interesting," he tossed out in answer.

He ran his eyes down the list of flowers and gulped when he came to honeysuckle. Frantically, he flipped to its page, and beneath a description, a sketch of the plant, and a summary of its various uses, Nicholas found, with trembling fingers, the sentiment it was said to express: "Boundless and devoted affection."

The book fell from the apprentice's hands.

"Mr. Pye's *Discourse on the Diseases of Cattle* has come in as well," Mr. Flinders continued. "You can find it next to his *Treatise on Swine*."

Nicholas hastily snatched up the book. "Excellent," he replied.

He turned again to the entry on honeysuckle, peering in awe at the message it bore and offering thanks to Mr. Quince, upon whose advice he'd opened his eyes—and beheld all about him an unsuspected world alive with signs and meanings.

" 'Boundless and devoted affection,' " he murmured to himself. Then suddenly Nicholas realized that he must reply to the message, and quickly. The public ball in

honor of the King would take place the following
night—a precious opportunity meant to be shared with
Juliana. But first he must reveal to her the receipt of
her message—and his own matching passion.

Briskly, Nicholas leafed through the book, seeking
the proper flower with which to convey his feelings to
Juliana.

"Hogg's *Commentaries on Luther* has also arrived," Mr.
Flinders noted.

Nicholas came to a sketch of a clump of Canterbury
bells—and stopped at once. He'd seen some growing
in a garden that morning. He noted its message, "Acknowledgment." It was appropriate, he told himself, but
something slightly stronger was needed.

"And a fine edition," the bookseller went on, "of
Coddington's *Commentaries on Hogg*."

"Truly," replied Nicholas absently.

He considered the cowslip, whose sentiment was "I
waste away without you." *Too* strong, he decided. He
mustn't affright her. Then he flipped to verbena, whose
message was "Enchantment"—and knew that his search
was over. Quickly, he read the flower's description: five
pink, red, or violet petals, toothed leaves, hairy stems.
Recalling that he was long overdue, he briefly studied
the sketch of the plant, replaced the book, thanked
Mr. Flinders, and hurried on to the shoe shop next door.

"Well, well!" crowed Mr. Quince from his bench.

"Look who's come through the door—*at last*."

Nicholas lowered his guilty eyes and speedily emptied his basket.

"Tell me, Zeph," said Mr. Quince, aiming a wink at his brawny journeyman. "Does the boy seem to have *grown* since he left?"

Zeph scratched at his grubby whiskers and clamped an eye on Nicholas. "I believe you're right, sir. Shot up like a beanstalk." He raised his mallet and returned to pounding the leather on his lapstone. "One more chore on his list of errands and I'm afraid he'd be stoopin' to get through the door."

Nicholas cast a glance at the doorway and Zeph let out a gravelly laugh.

"Your job's *making* shoes," barked Mr. Quince, "not wearing 'em out. Now to work with you, lad!"

The apprentice sat down and commenced beating leather, staring raptly across at his master, who was finishing up a shoe brought in for repair by Juliana herself. Dreamily Nicholas eyed the shoe's buckle, as if beholding in the glint of the brass the sparkle in Juliana's own eyes.

"And remember, lad! Alert as a hare—a hare with hounds at its heels!"

A butcher's wagon stopped in the street. Mr. Quince stepped out to inspect the meat while Nicholas endeavored, as best he could, to put a harelike look in his eyes.

"Spring be late this year, apprentice," boomed Zeph above the noise of their mallets.

"Yes, sir, it is," replied Nicholas.

In unison they pounded their lapstones, softening pieces of sturdy sole leather.

"Aye, the courtin' season be short." The journeyman grinned at Nicholas. "Not a moment to lose, lad!" he shouted out. "Take a lesson from Zeph—and be bold with the girls!"

He launched into whistling a merry tune. Then he stopped his pounding. Nicholas stopped too.

"Now take the case of our Mr. Quince." He leaned toward Nicholas and lowered his voice. "His suffering heart's in thrall to Miss Catchfly—and has been now for six full years!"

The apprentice gaped at Zeph in shock. Such an un-likely possibility, like that of the sun falling out of the sky or the oceans draining into the earth, had never before occurred to him.

"Why, that sulphur-tongued spinster would snatch up a suitor quick as a frog would a fly. And yet our master is *still* accumulating the courage to speak his heart to her, and has been ever since he first took her size— and beheld her delicate pair of feet!"

The journeyman burst out into a laugh and returned to beating his leather.

" 'Ethereal,' I've heard him call 'em. 'Fit for a god-dess.' 'The pinnacle of beauty.' Whispered to his workbench, mind you, instead of to the woman herself." He shook his head and returned to beating his leather. "Nay, boy, take your learning from Zeph. Don't dally about with the girls—be bold!"

He flashed a grin at Nicholas as Mr. Quince walked in, empty-handed.

"Poor-looking pickings?" Zeph inquired.

Mr. Quince heated a burnishing iron. "On the contrary, the meat was of the highest quality—if you were looking to make it into boots."

He rubbed the hot iron along the heel and sole of Juliana's shoe, vigorously bringing a gloss to the leather. Then Nicholas watched as Mr. Quince quickly applied a coat of tallow, dismayed that his master should handle the shoe with such familiarity, instead of the reverence it deserved.

"No, my lads, no meat I'm afraid. But Nicholas has guaranteed we shan't starve." Mr. Quince eyed the shoe, set it on a shelf, and lit his pipe with an ember. "That is, if our *dreamy-eyed* provider remembered to purchase bread at the bakery."

Nicholas pricked up his ears. "Yes, sir."

"And the sole knife the cutler repaired?"

"Yes, sir."

"And honey?"

"Yes, sir."

"And a half-dozen candles?"

Nicholas froze, panic-stricken.

"For the illumination tomorrow night?" Mr. Quince refreshed his memory.

Suddenly Nicholas recalled the words, licked his lips, and put down his lapstone.

"I'll fetch 'em right this instant, sir! And be back as quick as—"

"Back to your pounding!" Mr. Quince aimed his pipe at Nicholas. "You'll do no more expeditioning about until you've finished a full day's work!"

Reluctantly, Nicholas returned to his leather. He longed for a chance to pick some verbena, present it to an awestruck Juliana, and arrange to meet the next night at the ball. Contemplating this course of action, he waxed a shoe, mixed lamp soot and egg white, blacked two boots, warmed glue for his master, was instructed in the art of carving a last, was told the grim tale of a *daydreaming* apprentice whose last was too small and whose shoes were too tight and whose unspeakable end might serve as a warning—and finally was released out the door, with money for candles in his pocket.

He hurried down the walk, then stopped. He knew there were candles at Miss Stubbin's shop. But where could he find what was more important—a bouquet of verbena for Juliana?

Frantically Nicholas glanced about. And suddenly it occurred to him that verbena might not grow in Charleston, or might be only exceedingly rare. It could take him days to find some, or weeks—unless he chanced to search the right spot. Disheartened, he turned a circle in the street, wondering which point of the compass to follow. Then something caught the apprentice's eye and he tilted his gaze to the copper image of Saint Crispin, whose hammer glinted in the sun—and at once he knew where to point his feet.

After all, Saint Crispin watched over him—Mr. Quince himself had told him so. It could therefore hardly be accidental that among the eagles and angels and roosters and the rest of the mixed flock of weathervanes only Saint Crispin faced north at the moment. On the contrary, he reasoned, the meaning was clear. The saint knew where verbena grew—and was showing him the way.

Nicholas squeezed the nutmeg in his pocket and set off in line with Saint Crispin's hammer. He scanned every window box he passed. He surveyed every yard and every garden, and drew up beside an iron fence. On the other side he spied violet flowers. Squatting down to inspect them more closely, he remembered the description he'd read of verbena, stuck his nose between the bars, and all of a sudden drew back. The petals were the proper color but the leaves were broad, not thin like verbena's, and Nicholas quickly moved on down the street, dreading to think of presenting the wrong flower and inadvertently shouting out some blasphemy in the language of petals.

Block after block he walked along, while the afternoon shadows stretched out toward the east. Sighing, he turned and sighted Saint Crispin, continued on—and then stopped.

He got down on his knees and studied a clump of flowers growing beside a brick walk. The petals were violet, five to the flower. The stems were hairy. The leaves were toothed. In wonder, Nicholas realized he was staring at verbena.

Stealthily, he looked around, dug out his jackknife, and cut four stalks. Then he sprang to his feet and turned a corner, muttering thanks to his patron saint.

Grinning, he darted down the street. He stopped at Miss Stubbin's shop for candles, then struck out toward Miss Catchfly's grocery. Picturing the potent effect his bouquet would have on Juliana, the apprentice spotted the shop just ahead and anxiously hurried his steps. He smiled to think of the girl's surprise, cleared his throat, put his hand on the door latch, pressed down his thumb—and found the door stuck. Desperately, he jiggled the latch. Then he raced to his right, peered through a window—and realized that the shop was closed.

Stunned, he glanced at the sinking sun. He'd hardly noticed the lateness of the hour. And with a holiday on the following day, Miss Catchfly had no doubt closed up early.

Nicholas cast a last look through the window, then

moved down the street at a despondent pace. The shop, he knew, would be closed the next day. And although he'd chanced to see Juliana arrive at the grocery early one morning, where she lived was a mystery. Yet somehow he had to find her—and soon. A problem he gnawed on unceasingly while he returned to the shoe shop, put the flowers in water, ate supper, and finally climbed into bed.

3

A mockingbird burst into song from a treetop and Nicholas shook off a dream and sat up. Startled to find the sun long risen, he threw on his clothes, dashed toward the stairway, prepared to face Mr. Quince below—and recalled that it was a holiday.

Relieved, he wandered drowsily downstairs. The shop was silent and would stay that way, though the door was unlocked for anyone with shoes or boots to be picked up—and instantly Nicholas spun around and stared at Juliana's shoe.

Mr. Quince had finished repairing it. And he'd told Juliana when she'd brought it in that he'd have it done by the holiday. No doubt she'd stop in to get it that morning—and the apprentice beamed to realize that the problem of hunting her down was solved.

Reverently, he picked up the shoe, running a finger along the brass buckle and over the glossy black leather. Then it crossed his mind that Juliana might, by chance, have forgotten about it. Or perhaps she wouldn't have time to retrieve it until the day *after* the ball.

His spirits wilted. He put the shoe down, knowing he couldn't be certain that she'd come to the shop in time. Working his brain for a way to find her, he found himself absently eyeing a hammer—and suddenly remembered Saint Crispin.

Jubilant, Nicholas charged upstairs, seized the verbena, and scurried back down, sure that Saint Crispin, his guide and protector, would show him the way to Juliana.

"Good day to you, Nicholas," smiled Mr. Quince, entering the shop from the kitchen. "Fine weather for the militia to march, is it not?"

Nicholas halted and looked out the window. "Yes, sir," he answered. Then he ran for the doorway.

"You too like to watch the review, do you lad?"

Nicholas froze with his hand on the latch. "Yes, sir." He shuffled his feet impatiently.

"Well then, no doubt I'll see you there."

"No doubt," he replied, and rushed through the door.

He sped down the walk, then looked up at the vane. It had shifted direction during the night and Nicholas found that it now faced south. Orienting himself accordingly, the apprentice set off down the street, his eyes alert for Juliana.

He wondered whether she'd turn a corner and suddenly appear in his path. Or perhaps he'd catch just the merest glimpse of her face in a second-story window. Glancing about, wary as a hunter, Nicholas abruptly stopped.

He lowered his eyes, viewing a patch of verbena growing beneath a rosebush, along the wall of a church. Deciding the four stalks he'd brought along hardly made a proper bouquet, he squatted down and pulled out his jackknife.

"*You,* boy! Rascal! Away from those flowers!"

It was a woman's voice, half a block behind him. Fearing to turn around and be seen, Nicholas quickly shot to his feet, ripping the back of his shirt on a rose thorn, and burst into flight down the street.

Leaving a trail of verbena petals, he sprinted until his sides ached, then stopped. He looked behind him, and saw he was safe. Catching his breath, he tidied his hair and assessed the lengthy rip in his shirt. He hadn't had time to pick more flowers—his scanty bouquet would have to do.

Watchfully, the apprentice pushed on, following the street until it ended at a park running along the water. Unable to travel any farther in the direction Saint Crispin had pointed him, Nicholas struck out down a path to his left, aware of diverging from his course but reasoning that to explore the park was no doubt what the saint had meant him to do.

Eyes skinned, he marched along. The path was crowded with people strolling and taking in the view of the sea. Yet after walking from one end to the other without catching sight of Juliana, Nicholas began to wonder whether Saint Crispin might have pointed south for some other reason or some other shoemaker. Resting himself, he leaned against a tree. And all of a sudden he saw her.

She was alone, gazing glumly at the water, musing on the inconstancy of the villainous Winthrop Whistlewood.

The apprentice stared at her in awe. His heart broke into a trot, then a gallop. Intending to surprise her with his bouquet, he hid the flowers behind his back, licked his lips, breathed in deeply, and stepped up quietly behind her.

"Excuse my intruding on—"

"Mercy!" she cried. She whirled about, pale as skimmed milk. "Such a fright!" She blinked and gasped for breath.

"Forgive me," fumbled Nicholas. "Please."

He looked down, and suddenly realized that his entire supply of words had fled his mind like a frightened flock of birds. Trembling, Nicholas glanced around, ransacked his brain for something to say, and finally, in desperation, mutely thrust the bouquet at Juliana.

"Scoundrel!" she muttered between her teeth. For behind the apprentice she spied the figure of Winthrop Whistlewood strolling her way—in the company of his latest sweetheart.

"I'm afraid I must go at once," she announced. Having decided that morning never to look on the face of her former suitor again, she lowered her eyes, turned briskly around, and bustled away from the baffled Nicholas.

Astonished, he watched her vanish from sight. Had he said something wrong? Was his manner too forward? Had she noticed the rip in the back of his shirt? He stared at the bouquet in his hand, wondering what had become of its magic.

He set off toward the shoe shop, then slowed to a stop.

There were petals on the ground—verbena petals. The very ones, the apprentice suspected, that had fallen when he'd streaked down the street.

In horror he gaped at his bouquet. No wonder Juliana had fled! Verbena might signify "Enchantment"—but verbena had *five* petals to the flower. Having sat overnight, then been shaken about, his verbena had lost so many petals that she'd taken it to be something else!

Terror-stricken, he threw down the flowers and darted

to Mr. Flinders' bookshop.

"Nicholas, my scholar—step right in!" Mr. Flinders lowered the book he was reading. "The shop is closed, you understand. Except, of course, for those like you— those who crave knowledge as others crave food."

Nicholas rushed toward the volume he sought, pulled it out, and opened it up, determined to find out what message Juliana had read in his bouquet.

"You'll be very interested to know, I'm sure, that the Reverend Picklewaite's *Reply to Doubt* has arrived in my most recent shipment."

"Truly," Nicholas mumbled in answer. He searched the book for another flower resembling verbena but with fewer petals, and came to a stop at the madder plant. It too was said to have narrow leaves and violet petals—*four* to the flower. Fearfully, Nicholas scanned its description, read the account of its various uses, and came at last to the message it bore: "Vicious accusation."

The apprentice whitened.

"Indeed," said the bookseller. "Plus the Reverend's extremely popular *Cure for Noxious Curiosity*."

Nicholas quickly slammed the book shut, as if to extinguish the memory of the error.

"I must see it sometime," he stuttered in reply.

Too mortified to track Juliana and attempt to explain the mistake to her, he shuffled weakly out of the store and into the shoe shop, where he slumped in a chair.

"Ho there, apprentice," Zeph called out, stepping grandly down the stairs. "Look up and cast your eyes on your comrade—a mere journeyman at making shoes, but a master craftsman at courting."

Nicholas found Zeph scrubbed and shaved, clothed in a clean pair of breeches and a coat ablaze with copper buttons.

"Aye, feast your eyes—and remember. No time to dally. Be bold with 'em, boy! And mark me, if I don't have a woman's arm in mine by sundown you can call me a dew-eared, fumble-fingered apprentice at the art of love."

Gaily, Zeph strutted out the door, while Nicholas pondered his troubles. He considered the journeyman's counsel a moment, but the thought of boldly addressing Juliana, after his accidental insult, was too terrifying to contemplate. Yet somehow he had to convince her of his true feelings before the ball that evening—and all of a sudden he remembered her shoe.

He turned and snatched it up off the shelf. There was still a chance she'd come for it before the ball began. And although he feared to approach her in person, he realized he could write her a note, stick it inside, and hope she'd find it.

Quickly Nicholas searched out a quill, a bottle of ink, and a piece of paper. Knowing the note was his only hope, he decided to take Zeph's advice and be bold, and at once he recalled the flowery phrases Zeph had reported Mr. Quince to whisper in reference to Miss Catchfly's feet.

"You are the pinnacle of loveliness," the apprentice neatly wrote out. "Your ethereal beauty fills my thoughts. I regard you as I would a goddess."

Nicholas considered the note, sure that such potent words as those would outweigh the morning's mishap.

"I shall attend the militia review this afternoon," he continued, "in hope of finding you. Allow me to regain your precious favor." He paused, then remembered Mr. Flinders' phrase. "Which I crave as others crave food."

Since the author of the message would be obvious, Nicholas didn't sign his name, and after waiting for the ink to dry he folded the paper, picked up the shoe, polished its brass buckle with his sleeve, and tucked the note inside.

The apprentice pulled the nutmeg from his pocket. If Juliana attended the review, it would mean that she'd forgiven him. And if she'd forgiven him, he could bear to approach her and propose that they meet at the ball that night. Ardently praying for such an outcome, he put the nutmeg to his nose, sniffed it deeply—and saw the door burst open.

"I demand to see Mr. Quince at once!" The speaker was none other than Miss Catchfly, and Nicholas hurriedly hid the nutmeg in his pocket, just as his master entered.

"My *dear* Miss Catchfly—how good to see you." He

closed the kitchen door behind him and gazed at her adoringly.

"You'll change your mind about *that* soon enough!"

In a rage, she produced a pair of shoes and slammed them down on a bench.

"The tacks—they're driving up into my heel! One more minute of wearing and I'd have never been able to pull them off!"

Mr. Quince examined one of the shoes. Anxiously, the apprentice looked on, wishing he could somehow disappear like smoke up a chimney.

"Tell me, Nicholas," said Mr. Quince. "Did you not attach these particular heels?"

"Yes, sir," the apprentice mumbled.

"And did you realize at the time that the tacks happened to be a size too long?"

Nicholas cleared his throat. "No, sir."

"Leatherhead!" spat out Miss Catchfly. "Idiot!"

Mr. Quince answered her scowl with a smile. "The boy's new to the trade, you understand. Still learning to follow in the steps of Saint Crispin, patron saint of cobblers."

"And scoundrels!" Fiercely, Miss Catchfly glared at the shoemaker. "I demand the shoes be repaired at once—before they make a martyr of *me*."

"But madam, it being a holiday for the lad—"

"Aye, so he and the rest can wander free as pigs,

getting into mischief! Why just this morning I scared off a boy about to steal a fistful of flowers."

Nicholas froze stiff as a fencepost.

"The brazen rascal," responded Mr. Quince.

"From the front of a church!" Miss Catchfly added. "*That* be the sort of villainy that holidays from work will lead to."

Terrified that she'd recognize him, Nicholas turned his back to her and headed quietly for the stairs.

"Aye—and *that* be the boy right there! With the rip running down the back of his shirt!"

Nicholas halted. He felt for the rip, and cursed himself to recollect that he'd only been spotted from behind.

"Nicholas!" boomed Mr. Quince. "Is this so?"

The apprentice lowered his eyes. "Yes, sir."

His master stared at him in shock. "Upstairs with you, boy, and change your shirt! Then you'll come back down and devote the rest of the afternoon to Miss Catchfly's shoes—putting a brand-new heel on each, to remember your carelessness by."

Mr. Quince smiled across at Miss Catchfly while Nicholas shuddered, recalling the note.

"But sir—the militia review! I'd arranged—"

"The comfort of our customers' feet comes first—remember that, boy. Now be off!"

Sulkily, Nicholas climbed the stairs. He made out the sound of the militia's drums and calculated it would take three hours at the least to finish Miss Catchfly's shoes. By the time he was through the review would be over—and his last chance to speak to Juliana would be gone.

Slowly, Nicholas changed his shirt, bitterly eyeing the rip from the rose thorn and wishing he'd never heard of verbena. Stepping reluctantly down the stairs, he saw that Miss Catchfly had departed, watched as his master left for the review, and realizing that the note he'd written to Juliana must be removed, turned toward the shelf—and found the shoe gone.

A chill scurried up the apprentice's spine. Madly, he combed the shop for the shoe—then suddenly he knew what had happened. While he'd leisurely put on another shirt, Juliana must have happened by, picked up her shoe, and quickly left.

Desperately Nicholas rushed out the door. He peered up and down the street in a panic, but Juliana was nowhere in sight.

The apprentice felt the strength drain from his limbs. After reading the note, attending the review, and waiting in vain for him to appear, she'd conclude that he'd meant to make a fool of her—and would never set eyes upon him again!

In utter despair, he shuffled inside and turned to Miss Catchfly's shoes. Working slowly, unconcerned with the time, he gloomily took the heels apart, ignoring the sound of the militia marching only a few blocks away. He constructed a pattern, and from the heaviest cowhide laboriously cut out eight pieces of leather. Hardly aware of the hours passing, he built up the heels layer by layer, only dimly aware by the time he'd finished that the sound of drums had long ceased.

Nicholas stood up. He felt numb inside, and vowed to forget Juliana entirely. Putting Miss Catchfly's shoes on the shelf, he glanced about, wandered outside, and chanced to look up at the weathervane.

Saint Crispin was facing west at the moment, though a breeze butted Nicholas from the south. He recalled how the vane had faithfully led him to a patch of verbena and to Juliana. And having nothing better to do, he set off in a westerly direction, wondering what it was Saint Crispin held in store for him.

The streets were noisy with singing and shouting. Fire-crackers rang out in the distance. Nicholas stopped while a cart passed before him, pulled by a pair of blindered horses—and at once the apprentice's eyes lit up. He wondered if this could be the sight his patron saint had meant him to see—for his troubles would never have begun if he hadn't cast off his blinders, opened his eyes, and noticed the extra nutmeg.

Puzzling over Saint Crispin's intent, Nicholas pressed on farther to the west, caught a glimpse of the harbor, and halted. The saint, he suspected, had meant him to see the water, and suddenly the apprentice knew why. He must fling himself into the sea at once. Only that would solve his problems, and Nicholas anxiously turned toward the weathervane, wondering if this indeed was its meaning.

Horses and wagons hurried past, while men piled wood in the street for a bonfire. Nervously Nicholas scanned the harbor. He decided to push on a block or two farther, just in case he might have misinterpreted Saint Crispin—and looked up to find himself suddenly face to face with Juliana.

"Good day," she offered, stopping. "Again."

The apprentice paled. His heart bolted. She didn't seem to be angry, and in an instant he abandoned his vow to forget her and decided to right matters once and for all.

"Forgive me for not appearing!" he burst out.

The girl seemed amused. "Not appearing where?"

"At the militia review—this afternoon!"

Juliana gazed at Nicholas, baffled.

"As I'd promised you in the note."

"What note?"

"The note I tucked in your shoe, of course!"

"*What* shoe?"

Nicholas gaped in wonder.

"The brass-buckled shoe you brought in for repair— and picked up this very afternoon!" He fixed his eyes on her, then glimpsed the sight of Mr. Quince crossing the street—strolling arm in arm with Miss Catchfly.

"That?" cried Juliana, disbelieving. "But that shoe was Miss Catchfly's—she merely sent me to bring it in to be mended."

The apprentice stared at Mr. Quince as he and the woman he worshipped turned a corner and disappeared from view—and in a flash he knew what must have happened. While he'd been upstairs changing his shirt, Miss Catchfly had left the shop with her shoe and had read the note, devouring the praise the timid shoemaker had meant for her feet. And since it was Mr. Quince who must have handed her the shoe, she'd naturally assumed the note was from him—and had joyfully joined him at the review.

Marveling at this turn of events, Nicholas quickly realized that Juliana hadn't waited for him, and might still be disposed to look on him favorably.

"As for this morning," the apprentice sputtered, "it wasn't a bouquet of madder I'd brought you—"

Juliana cocked her head quizzically.

"I didn't mean 'vicious accusation' at all. It was *verbena* I'd picked, with *five* petals to the flower."

Juliana chuckled. "Does it make a great difference?"

Nicholas eyed her in disbelief.

"Why—the message," he faltered. "I'd brought verbena for the sentiment it carries—'Enchantment.' In reply to the honeysuckle you wore."

"In reply?" She appeared surprised at the notion. "And tell me. What message does honeysuckle bear?"

The apprentice gaped at her, dumbfounded.

"Why, 'Boundless and devoted affection'—of course!"

"Truly," she replied. "How very interesting."

Nicholas could hardly believe his ears.

"You were wearing some yesterday morning," he declared, as if pleading for his sanity. "The morning you gave me the extra nutmeg."

He produced the nutmeg and held it before her, the undeniable proof of her love.

"Extra?" The smile fled her lips.

"Don't you remember?" The apprentice trembled. "I ordered six—and you gave me seven!"

"*I* did that?" Juliana gasped, and quickly glanced about.

"I must have been half asleep," she whispered. "If Miss Catchfly knew, why she'd scald me and skin me!"

Nicholas slowly absorbed her confession—and struggled to steady his legs. He caught sight of Zeph, a block ahead, with a woman on his arm as promised. Staring cheerlessly at the couple, Nicholas put the nutmeg in his pocket and vowed never again to try his hand at the craft of love.

The cannons at Fort Johnson saluted the King. Sighing, the apprentice turned to go.

"As no doubt you know," Juliana spoke up, "there's a public ball to take place this evening. To honor the holiday, of course."

Nicholas, entombed in his gloom, hardly heard her words.

"I was wondering," she persevered, "if I might expect to find you there."

The bells of St. Michael's church rang out. Thunderstruck, the apprentice stopped.

"You don't seem at all like that odious Winthrop Whistlewood," Juliana shouted, straining to be heard above the pealing.

Dazed, Nicholas wondered vaguely whom it was she was speaking of. In disbelief he stared at her. He swallowed hard. He cleared his throat twice.

"Yes, of course," he announced over the chiming. "I thought that I—that I might attend."

A ship in the harbor boomed a salute. Firecrackers exploded nearby. His thoughts spinning dreamily, Nicholas turned, squinted his eyes, spied the copper image of Saint Crispin, and felt sure that this was what his patron saint had been pointing toward all along.

The Man
of Influence

1

LIGHTNING TWITCHED LIKE a dreaming dog's legs. The wind blew. Rain fell. And Zorelli lay awake in the night.

Wide-eyed, he listened to the beating rain, enduring each drop that struck the roof. He turned toward Marta, his wife, beside him. She was sleeping soundly, unaware of the weather, and he gazed at her with contempt. He himself had never found it possible to sleep on a rainy night.

Rain, after all, was the enemy of stone, pounding it finally into dust. And Zorelli was a stone carver by trade, a maker of monuments.

"Lolling in the doorway, letting in the cold." Marta looked up from scrubbing the floor, sighed wearily, and shook her head. "Come now, Zorelli—will that keep us fed?"

The sculptor ignored her and surveyed the sky, while his cat, Angelina, coiled about his ankles. The storm had passed over the rooftops of Genoa. The cobblestones glistened and the morning air was filled with the gaudy crowing of roosters.

"Is this any way to lure a patron?" Marta pleaded with her husband. "Unshaven, dressed in a filthy tunic, lurking about the doorway like a thief?"

A pair of mounted soldiers rode by. A fruit seller passed, pushing his cart. Zorelli looked down at Angelina, who cried and rubbed meaningfully against his legs. Stepping inside, he searched the kitchen and fed her the last scrap of cheese in the house.

"That cat of yours never lacks for food—but what of us?" asked Marta. "Already the mice have deserted the house. By tomorrow night we'll have nothing to gnaw on—unless, of course, you pick up your hammer and carve us a roast goose out of granite."

Zorelli glared at her in silence, then turned and stormed into his studio.

Restlessly, he paced the room. He was a powerful man, broad shouldered, proud chinned, and he settled himself at last on a stool, took note of the spotless floor, and sneered. It should have been littered with chips of stone. There ought to have been granite dust in the air. But commerce was bad, Genoa's harbor was still, and the mighty Boccas and Tarentinos, whose fleeting features Zorelli had transferred to statues of imperishable stone, no longer had money to spare for his skills. Even the ruling Ferrantes, his grandest patrons, seemed to have forgotten him.

In disgust, he gazed at his idle tools. If no commission came his way today he'd be forced to return to work at the quarry, toiling once again beside his loutish father and his foul-smelling brothers. And yet, Zorelli reflected, he was an intimate of the high-born now. He'd strolled down the halls of the cultured and rich, arranged them in poses, engaged them in talk. He jumped to his feet and strode outside, shuddering to think of descending once more to the coarse, sweaty company of the quarry.

Aimlessly, he roamed the town, walking briskly in the chill autumn air. Down a side street he caught a glimpse of the plaza and his mounted statue of Lorenzo Ferrante, Governor of Genoa, her leader in arms and great patron of culture. Zorelli paused, then marched ahead, savoring his link with the man.

He entered the swarming marketplace—and erupted in a rage when a man bumped him in passing. After all, he was no worthless commoner like the rest—his customers were persons of influence. His wares were no melons or stinking fish, but immortality itself!

He picked his way through the motley gathering. Vendors bellowed, pigs squealed. Beggars and thieves circulated like maggots. Zorelli struggled to escape the crowd, when all of a sudden a shout rang out. Chickens scattered, the throng parted, and Lorenzo himself, mounted on his steed, solemnly entered the market.

At last! thought Zorelli, straining for a view. In the midst of the rabble—a man worthy of stone!

Genoa's governor towered above the crowd, peering ahead with hawklike aloofness. Gazing in reverence upon the great man, Zorelli noticed his black cloak and hat and knew he must be bound for the grave of his nephew, the infant Alessandro, to pay his yearly respects.

Zorelli himself had carved the tomb for the child, who would have ruled the house of Ferrante, and therefore Genoa itself, had a window been shut and the prince not taken a chill one night and died.

Grimly, Lorenzo rode through the market. Zorelli longed to catch his attention, to be acknowledged and elevated above the rest. Like a sunflower, he slowly turned, devotedly facing Lorenzo as he passed, while the object of his veneration stared ahead, unaware of his presence.

Once again the noisy bargaining resumed. Scornfully, Zorelli regarded the crowd.

Mayflies! he swore. Creatures of a day! Never would their paltry lives earn preservation in stone!

He threaded his way through the multitude, stopping to watch two women haggle with a vendor over the price of a fish.

Beasts! hissed Zorelli. Concerned only with eating!

With relief he fled the marketplace, exalted with his lofty perspective. And yet—he passed a bakery and inhaled the scent of freshly baked bread—he too felt a sudden pang of hunger.

Cursing his stomach, he emptied his pockets to pay for a roll and stormed away.

That night Zorelli paced his studio long after Marta had climbed into bed. A restlessness grew up inside him whenever he wasn't swinging his hammer or exerting his files against stone.

He made up his mind to take a walk, stepped outside, and headed for the harbor. Angelina followed behind him.

"The night is black, is it not, Angelina?" The sculptor's cat was black as well and had disappeared upon entering the darkness like a fish thrown back to sea.

"The moon has yet to rise," said Zorelli. "But we know our way about, don't we now?"

Invisibly, Angelina followed beside him. It was late and they were alone in the streets. Gradually the salt air grew stronger, and soon the two of them reached the docks and wandered out to the end of a wharf.

"The waters are still tonight, Angelina." The waves lapped softly against the wharf. The few boats at anchor bobbed peacefully. Angelina sat and peered out to sea, sniffing the air with interest.

"And the stars!" The sculptor gazed up at the heavens. "Have you ever before beheld them so bright?"

"Never!" came a voice in reply.

At once Angelina hissed and fled. Zorelli whirled— and found himself facing the flickering image of what seemed to be a man.

"A pox on the stars!" continued the voice. *"Too* bright for my liking. Aye, blinding, they are!"

Zorelli studied the speaker in wonder. He was short legged and burly and missing an ear. Fitfully, he glowed and dimmed, as if he were made of starlight himself.

"You're Zorelli, the stone carver, if I'm not mistaken." His clothes were ragged and glimmered like their wearer, as if they were but the dying embers of their former selves.

"And who—or what—are you?" asked Zorelli.

"What *am* I?" The apparition snorted. "Why, a ghost! What *else* did you take me for?"

Zorelli stared at the spirit in awe, his hands fluttering like moths. He wondered where Angelina had gone, and had he not been trapped at the end of the wharf he would gladly have fled as well.

"And what brings you—here?" the sculptor stammered.

"What *brings* me here," said the specter, "is you."

Zorelli stiffened. "What is it you want?"

"Your services, naturally."

"What?" gasped Zorelli.

"I want to hire you. To fashion a statue."

Zorelli gaped at the ghost in amazement.

"I'm prepared to pay, you understand." He reached into a pocket and produced a coin purse.

"Twenty-five ducats now. Aye, and fifty more when you're finished."

Zorelli's eyes lit. Seventy-five ducats! No more would he have to return to the quarry! He could live for months on such a sum. And yet—he found himself staring at the coin purse.

"How can I be sure that the money—is real?"

The specter grinned and shook the purse, causing the coins to jingle brightly in proof of their substantiality.

Zorelli smiled. "Well now!" he spoke up. "And what manner of statue had you in mind? Something for a garden? A nymph, perhaps?"

The spirit peered into the stone carver's eyes. "I would have you carve the statue of me."

"Of *you*?" Zorelli froze in astonishment. He stared at the specter shimmering before him, a quantity of phosphorescence poured in the mold of a man.

"Naturally, I'm accustomed to dealing—with the living," Zorelli fumbled awkwardly. With growing revulsion he took note of the spirit's missing ear, his crooked teeth, and the long jagged rip down the front of his doublet. Had warm flesh belonged to him he might have been taken for a beggar, or a rag merchant dressed in his wares, and suddenly Zorelli wondered if the man was worthy of salvation in stone—or deserved forgetting, like most of humanity.

The sculptor turned his eyes toward the water.

"If I might be so bold," he asked delicately, "were you a man of any—*influence* while you lived?"

"I'm afraid I was," answered the specter.

Zorelli jerked in surprise—and relief. The man was of more account than appeared. Stone would not be misused.

"I—thought as much," mumbled the sculptor. He felt embarrassed at having asked the question and was flooded with a sudden respect for the spirit.

"Then again," said the ghost, "if you don't have the time—"

"Not at all!" Zorelli interrupted. "I should be honored, of course, to accept the task. Why, sitting at home I've a fine block of marble—what size of a statue had you in mind?"

"Life-size," the spirit answered gravely. "I wish to be shown just as I was."

"Fine!" The stonecarver beamed at having found himself a patron at last. "Naturally I'll dress you in the finest attire, whatever you—"

"No need for that," spoke the phantom. "I want to be shown in the clothes I have on. Aye, just as I looked that night."

Zorelli gaped at the ghost's worn-out shoes, wretched doublet, and rat-gnawed cap. "A man of influence dressed—in rags? Surely a fine, turbaned hat at the least—"

"As for the pose," continued the ghost, "see that you show me cradling an infant. Aye, and holding a cup to its lips."

Zorelli digested his words in dismay. He was accustomed to depicting his subjects triumphant, with swords upraised, in the midst of great deeds. But a man—feeding an infant in his arms?

The sculptor tried to compose himself. "Your child, of course—"

"Not at all," barked the spirit. "And at my feet, carve out a cat. Scrawny, with no left ear—just like me."

Zorelli started.

"A true friend, he was. Found him here by the water one winter, and as soon as I saw he was missing an ear—why, I knew we'd understand each other, and get along just fine."

Zorelli stood facing his patron, dumbfounded. His earlier enthusiasm had left, replaced by a strange unease.

"Of course, I'll need to sketch you," he said, as if hoping to talk the ghost out of the project. "Make studies and drawings, you understand."

The spirit noticed the rising moon and seemed anxious to retreat from its light.

"Tomorrow night, then. Here. The same time."

He handed the coin purse to Zorelli, who opened it quickly to inspect the money. By the time he'd assured himself and looked up, his patron had disappeared.

2

The sun rose, devouring the frost on the ground, and Zorelli rolled out of bed.

Suddenly he remembered the ghost. He wondered if he had dreamed of the meeting. Then he reached for his tunic—and plucked out the coin purse.

He darted to a window and examined the coins. They were gold. He weighed one in his hand. It seemed to be real enough.

He hid the purse, then rushed out the door and down the street to a bakery.

"A loaf of bread!" the sculptor called out, above the din of the other customers.

A sow-faced baker fetched him a loaf. Cautiously, the stone carver held out one of the coins he'd received from the spirit—and watched in wonder as the man snatched it up, quickly returned him his change, and moved on.

For a moment Zorelli stood there, speechless, staring at the coins in his palm.

"And what's the matter with you?" snapped the baker. "A complaint with my counting?"

"Not at all!" said Zorelli.

"Step aside, then! Let the customers through!"

Smiling to himself, Zorelli scurried home.

"And where did you get money for bread?" asked Marta, eyeing the loaf in amazement.

Zorelli hungrily tore off a hunk. "Just where you would expect!" he replied. "I'm a sculptor. And I've been engaged by a patron!"

Victoriously, he marched into his studio.

"A patron?" Marta called after him. "Who?"

Zorelli stopped. She would never believe him.

"A man," he faltered. "A man—of some note."

He turned, relieved to find her absorbed in devouring a chunk of bread. Looking down at the piece in his own hand, he marveled that something so dense and substantial had resulted from so airy a being.

The sculptor filled his belly with bread, then sharpened his chisels one by one. He inspected his mallets, his rasps, his rifflers, his gouges and points, compass and square. Reverently, he cleaned his tools, then struggled with the block of marble, sliding it into the center of the room.

He gazed at it, patiently searching it for the proper pose of man, child, and cat. In his eyes the stone lost its solidity. It was fluid as quicksilver, a river of shapes. Pensively, he walked around it. From his stool, he stared at it for hours. He regarded it from near and far. And he waited for darkness to come.

"No shortage of stars in the sky tonight!"

Zorelli spun around. Down the wharf came the spirit, flickering as if concocted of fireflies.

"Aye, they pain my eyes, they do! If I had me a long-handled candle snuffer, such as would reach—why, I'd put 'em all out. Believe me I would—and hang a cloak on the moon!"

Zorelli stared at him, awed afresh to find himself in the employ of what was nothing more than the residue of a life, a cloud of ash, a burnt wick of a man.

"You wanted to draw me," spat out the ghost. "And

I'm here. So let's get on with it!"

The waters whispered. A sea gull squawked. Zorelli produced parchment and charcoal and commenced to sketch, by his subject's own light.

He eyed the ghost's teeth, crooked and sparse, leaning like tombstones in a forgotten graveyard. With mounting unease, he duly recorded his broken nose and the scar down his throat, longing for the smooth skins and noble features to which he was accustomed.

"As for your—ear," he spoke up with difficulty. "Naturally a hat, tilted to one side—"

"Never! I won't have you covering it up. I want to be exposed for just what I am. Or rather, for what I *was*—that night."

Distastefully Zorelli sketched the ear, hurrying over its ragged border.

"Seventeen years it's been that way." The spirit gazed out over the harbor. "Aye, since I first took up with the Boccas."

The Boccas! Zorelli brightened at the name. Spice merchants, they were, wealthy and refined. Zorelli himself had carved busts of the children, and he swelled with a sudden respect for his patron, as for all who lived in the world of the great.

"You were associated with the Boccas?" he asked.

"I should say! Seven years I served 'em."

Zorelli sketched the ghost's tattered doublet, wishing he could ignore the ragged tear that ran down the front.

"In what—*capacity* did you serve?" grinned the stone carver. "That is, if I may presume to ask."

"Commerce," said the ghost.

"Commerce?"

"That's right." He fingered his ear. "So to speak."

Zorelli wondered at his patron's meaning but hesitated to press him further.

"Aye, but that was long ago," the spirit mused, scanning the water. "Even before I'd met Tarentino."

"The Tarentinos, of course!" beamed Zorelli. He'd once carved a statue of Vito Tarentino, the government diplomat.

"A family of means," boasted the sculptor. "And magnificent learning as well!"

He sketched his patron's stumpy legs, imperceptibly lengthening them, as befitted a personage of his evident rank.

"It was the old man—Vito—I worked for," said the spirit. "Back when he was stationed in Florence."

"Truly!" Zorelli gawked, impressed. "And what, if I might ask, was your work?"

"Matters of state," the ghost answered back.

"Really, now."

"Right," said the spirit. "In a matter of speaking, you understand."

Zorelli sketched the ghost's battered shoes, pondering his words. To whom was he offering shelter in stone? Trembling, he regarded the ghost's tattered outfit, his broken nose and unsettling ear, and wished he'd never accepted his gold. But what was he to do—return to the quarry? After all, the spirit claimed to have been a man of influence while he'd lived, a point to which Zorelli clung like a cat.

"When can you have it finished?" asked the ghost.

"A month," Zorelli replied. "At the soonest."

"Fine!" He fingered the rip in his doublet. "Aye, a great relief it'll be. Just remember—down at my feet, a cat. One eared, and looking up at me. I want him to see for himself. See it plain."

Zorelli rolled up his sheet of parchment.

"When it's done," said the ghost, "put it in a wagon and take the road to Rompoli, by night."

The ghost set off.

"But wait!" cried Zorelli. "Where do I deliver it— and what of the payment? The other fifty ducats you promised!"

"I'll meet you along the way," said the spirit, and disappeared down the wharf.

3

Outside Zorelli's door, sun followed storm. The trees dropped their leaves. Voices passed by. Of these, however, he remained unaware. The statue alone absorbed his attention.

All day and deep into the nights he labored, working by sunlight, then candles and lamps. He joyed in stretching his muscles again, exulted in swinging his ringing hammer. Streams of sweat ran down his throat as if he were stoking the sun's own fires, and when he could work no more he fell into bed, exhausted and satisfied.

"What's your opinion, Angelina?" the sculptor addressed his cat one day. He glanced from her to the cat he was carving. "A fine beginning, wouldn't you say?"

Zorelli stepped back and studied the statue. The stocky form of the ghost had emerged, but the cat still lay hidden within the marble. The stone clung to the figure like a fog, and the sculptor reached for a chisel, took up his hammer, and returned to dispersing it.

"Tell me, Angelina," said Zorelli. "Have you ever seen such a statue before?"

The cat remained still, asleep in the sun.

"Never!" replied Marta, looking on from the doorway.

She stepped into the studio and eyed the marble. "A statue—commissioned by a beggar in rags?"

Zorelli swallowed. "Marta, I assure you—"

"What then—a thief? Or a murderer, perhaps?" She smiled knowingly at her husband. "Do you take me for a fool? No such patron exists! Amusing yourself in marble, you are—and *stealing* the money you give me for food."

"Marta, let me explain—"

"Explain?" She glared at the stone carver acidly. "All that I need to have explained is what possessed you to carve such a figure—and ruin a perfectly good block of marble!"

She swept out of the room, leaving the sculptor contemplating the statue and its subject.

Never, he mused, had he carved such a face. The barbarous mouth was that of a cutthroat. The eyes belonged to a hangman—or his prey. With each hammer blow he grew more afraid of the figure gradually being revealed.

And yet, Zorelli reminded himself, the man was acquainted with the wealthy Boccas, and the cultured Tarentinos as well. And he certainly hadn't lacked for money. Perhaps, he reasoned, *all* ghosts looked as grubby as this one—even the ghosts of the great.

He tried to drive the specter from his mind, picked up his hammer, and returned to work, musing on the power he possessed to fix the world's memory on a man for the length of the life of stone. Pounding, scraping, sanding, polishing, he gloried afresh in his ability to rescue his subjects from oblivion, securing for himself, parasitelike, a portion of their immortality.

Day by day the hammers became lighter, the chisels smaller, the files finer. Chipping gave way to grinding,

then sanding, each tool removing the marks of its prede-
cessor.

And then, one day, the statue was finished.

"Tell me—what do you think, Angelina?" Zorelli
picked her up and approached the figure who held a
cup to an infant, watched by a one-eared cat. "Come
now, let me hear your opinion."

Desperately, she jumped from his arms.

That afternoon the stonecarver hired a pair of horses
and a wagon, and with the help of three other brawny
men loaded the statue into the back. When evening fell,
he snapped the reins and headed down the road to Rompoli.

The night was still, the wintry air bare. The sky over-
head was littered with stars. For an hour he drove among
frost-stricken fields, wondering just where it was he was
headed—when suddenly he sighted a shimmer ahead.

"Well met!" grinned the ghost, approaching the
wagon. "You brought the statue, then?"

"There in the back."

"Fine!" beamed the spirit. "Finally! Aye, a great relief
it'll be."

He climbed aboard, glowing unreally, as if he were
but a magician's illusion.

"How much farther?" Zorelli asked.

"Oh, we've a bit of a ways," smiled the spirit.

Zorelli gave the reins a shake, sharing none of his

patron's good cheer. He glanced at the ghost's filthy
attire and shuddered at the thought of how his patron
must have stunk while he was alive. Even in stone such
a man would draw flies. And yet, he claimed to have
been of some importance. . . .

"You mentioned before your connection with the
Boccas," Zorelli spoke up hesitantly. "Engaged in the
spice commerce, didn't you say?"

"That's right," his companion answered back.

"Master of the countinghouse, were you? Or captain
of a ship, perhaps?" The sculptor smiled hopefully.

"Not likely. The competition was my job."

"The competition?"

"Right," said the spirit. "Making sure no other pesky
traders reached port with a load of pepper before us."
He reached absently for his missing ear. "And trying
to stay alive in the bargain."

The smile deserted Zorelli's lips. He studied the specter. Was he speaking of foul play? Naturally, he'd heard
of such things—but the polished Boccas? The thought
was absurd.

Nervously Zorelli clutched the reins, guiding the
wagon down the road toward its unknown destination.

"I recall that you mentioned working with Vito Tarentino as well," he spoke up. "Employed in matters of
state, I believe."

"Aye, matters of state," said the ghost.

Zorelli smiled respectfully. "Of what sort—if I may be so bold?"

"Finding out," said the spirit matter-of-factly.

"Finding out?"

"That's right," the ghost replied. "Whatever the old man wanted to know. Listening behind doors, searching rooms, paying the servants for what they knew. Aye, he kept me busy, he did."

Zorelli stared at the specter in shock. Tarentino, the renowned thinker and statesman—secretly engaging spies? Surely this mist of a man was lying. And yet, the sculptor asked himself, why should a ghost depart from the truth?

"Turn off to the left there," commanded the spirit. "Aye, that's where my poor bones be."

"Your bones?" said Zorelli. "Why here, of all places?"

"*I* wasn't consulted in the matter," snapped the ghost.

Zorelli guided the horses off the road and into a rocky meadow.

"Dead ahead, there. Aye, that's the spot."

The wagon banged and bounced over the ground, till Zorelli brought it at last to a halt.

"Fine!" exclaimed the spirit, hopping down. "The earth being soft as it is from the rains, I thought you could tip out the statue feet first and let it plant itself in the ground."

Zorelli climbed into the bed of the wagon, anxious to be rid of the statue and its subject. He breathed in deeply, and with the sum of his strength shoved the sculpture along the bed till it teetered, swung upright, and plunged into the earth.

"Well done," cheered the spirit. "Well done, indeed." Smiling, he studied the statue before him, running his fingers over the forms.

"Perfect!" he whispered. "Already I can feel it!" Blissfully, he gazed at the marble.

"Is this to be—your gravestone?" asked Zorelli.

"In a manner of speaking," murmured the spirit. He reached into a pocket, pulled out a coin purse, and handed it to Zorelli.

"The rest of your payment. You'll find it all there."

Zorelli watched, flattered and awed, as the ghost returned his gaze to the statue. Mounting the wagon and grabbing the reins, the sculptor felt suddenly loath to leave.

"If I might ask but one question," Zorelli spoke up. "Why was it you wished to be shown feeding an infant?"

The spirit turned. "I wasn't *feeding* the tyke." He fixed his eyes on the stone carver. "On the contrary, I was murdering it."

"*Murdering?*" gasped Zorelli.

"That's right. The cup I put to its lips held poison." Zorelli stared at the ghost, speechless. He felt sud-

denly weak. His hands took to trembling. A *murderer—*
celebrated in stone? Stone that he, Zorelli, had carved?

"Whatever—possessed you," stammered the sculptor,
"to pay to have such a scene depicted?"

The specter smiled. "A peaceful sleep. I was murdered
myself, you see, that same night. Before I had time to
get home to my cat and properly confess my crime."

Zorelli's thoughts whirled. "The cat?"

"That's right." The spirit's eyes brightened. "The one
you carved. Oh, he was a fine companion, and whenever
I did something that troubled my sleep—why, I told
him about it. Aye, and slept sound."

Zorelli's gaze rested on the cat, then slowly traveled
up the statue.

"And the infant?" he faltered, struggling with the
words.

"Just six months old. Alessandro, they called him."

"His full name!" the stone carver demanded, determined to know the full truth of the crime.

"Alessandro Ferrante."

The sculptor paled. "Lorenzo's nephew?"

"Aye, that's him."

"Impossible!" Zorelli jumped to the ground. "He
died of a cold! A chill in the night! I carved the tomb
for the child myself!"

The specter snorted. "A chill, was it now?" He
grinned, revealing his crooked teeth. "It was Lorenzo

himself who paid me to do it. Paid me those ducats I gave to you." He glanced at the rip down the front of his doublet. "And him who had me stabbed, as well."

In disbelief, Zorelli plucked out the coin purse and gaped at it in horror.

"Lorenzo Ferrante?" he murmured hypnotically. Wide-eyed, the stone carver stared at the coin purse, begging to disbelieve his own words.

"Aye," the ghost chuckled. "That's the one."

Zorelli stood motionless. He felt chilled and stiff, as if his own flesh were turning to stone.

Slowly, he climbed back onto the wagon and settled his gaze on the ghost. This then was his claim to influence, the sculptor numbly realized—to have made Lorenzo master of Genoa. Dazed and disoriented, Zorelli finally took up the reins, shook them, and left the ghost behind.

As if spellbound, the stone carver bounced along. While he entered Genoa the moon rose in the east, illuminating the Boccas' mansion, before which Zorelli paused awhile. It lit the Tarentinos' villa as well, where the sculptor halted once again. He passed the fine homes of his other fine patrons, then brought the wagon to a stop at the plaza. In the stillness he gazed at his statue of Lorenzo, astride his steed, glowing in the moonlight.

Shaking the reins, he drove on to the harbor. And there the sculptor climbed down from the wagon, shuffled out to the end of a wharf, and dropped the coin purse into the sea.

Ruing stone's durability, he scanned the horizon, and smiled to see clouds. Then he turned around, walked back to the wagon, mounted, and urged the horses homeward. And that night Zorelli the stone carver fervently prayed for rain.